Bill and Ben The Flowerpot Men Storybook

Illustrations by Anne Matthews

Contents

A catalogue record for this book is available from the British Library.

First edition

Published by Ladybird Books Ltd Loughborough Leicestershire UK
Ladybird Books Inc Auburn Maine 04210 USA

Printed in England (3)

Bill and Ben's market stall

When the man who works in the garden went home, Little Weed called out, "WEED! WEED!" and the Flowerpot Men came out of their flowerpots.

They found that the man who works in the garden had left two logs and a plank of wood beside their flowerpots.

"We can make a market stall," said Bill. "The logs can be the legs and the plank will make a counter. You go and find some things to sell, Ben."

Ben went into the garden shed and found a piece of bread, some old seeds and an apple, which he put on the counter. Bill made a little pile of the seeds, and Ben made crumbs with the piece of bread.

Their first customer was a blackbird. "I would like a piece of apple, please," he said.

Then a robin flew down. “What’s going on here?” he asked.

“We have a market stall,” said Bill. “Would you like something?”

“A piece of apple and some crumbs, please,” said the robin.

A thrush flew down to the market stall. “I think it’s my turn next,” she said. “Could I have some of those seeds?”

“Of course you can,” said Ben. He liked having a market stall because all the birds in the garden came to visit.

"This is very nice," said the blackbird. "It's just like a party."

"I love parties," said the robin. "Shall we all sing?"

The birds all started to whistle. Bill and Ben flobbadobbed, and Little Weed sang at the top of her voice.

"Let's have a market day every week," chirped the robin.

"But we couldn't come in the summer when we all have our babies to look after," said the thrush. "We are much too busy."

"That's all right," said Bill and Ben, "we'll have our market in the spring, autumn and winter."

"It would be very useful in the winter when the ground is hard and it's difficult to find anything to eat," said the blackbird, and they all agreed.

"I'm very hot and thirsty after all that singing," whispered Little Weed. So Bill and Ben fetched the watering can and gave Little Weed a long cool drink of water.

When the birds had eaten all the things from the stall, Bill and Ben

made everything tidy. But before they had time to lift the plank off the logs, Little Weed called out, "WEED! WEED!" because the man who works in the garden was coming back.

Bill and Ben had to scramble quickly into their flowerpots.

"That's funny," said the man. "I don't remember putting the plank on those logs."

But *we* know who did it, don't we?

Teddy learns to count

One day Teddy asked Andy Pandy, "What is three?"

"It's a number," replied Andy Pandy. "One, two, *three*."

"I know," said Teddy, "but I haven't three of anything. I've one nose, one mouth, two eyes and two ears, but I haven't a three."

Andy Pandy couldn't think of a three – only if you say one chin, one nose and one mouth all together make three. "But you do have four fingers on your hand and with the thumb that makes five," he said.

"I haven't any fingers, so I can't count that way," said Teddy.

"Yes you can. I'll show you how," said Andy Pandy. And he fetched a pair of gloves and put them on Teddy's paws.

"Now you can count one, two, three, four, five."

Teddy was very pleased, and he counted on one glove again and again. Then he asked, "What do I count on the other glove?"

"Six, seven, eight, nine, ten," replied Andy Pandy. "I know a song about numbers..."

Andy Pandy's counting song

One, two, three, four, five,
Once I caught a fish alive.
Six, seven, eight, nine, ten,
Then I let it go again.

Why did you let it go?
Because it bit my finger so.
Which finger did it bite?
This little finger on my right.

"I like that song," said Teddy. "But what is right?"

"It's your right hand," said Andy Pandy. "One hand is called right and the other is called left. You have a right and left foot, too. When you go marching, you say
left right, left right."

“Let’s march,” said Teddy. And he went to find his drum and Andy Pandy’s trumpet. Then they marched round and round the room singing their counting song.

“I would like to sing it to Looby Loo,” said Andy Pandy, and he went to fetch her.

While Andy Pandy was away, Teddy looked for another pair of gloves. He rummaged in Andy Pandy's cupboard and made it very untidy, and scattered things all over the floor.

At last he found another pair of gloves and put them on his feet. "Now I can count five on my left hand and five on my right hand,

five on my left foot and five on my right foot!"

"Yes, you are a clever little bear!" said Andy Pandy, crossly. "But you can tidy up all this mess before we do any more counting!"

Looby Loo's song

Andy Pandy's friend Looby Loo has a special song. Can you sing it with her?

Chorus (to follow each verse)

Here we go Looby Loo,
Here we go Looby Light,
Here we go Looby Loo,
All on a Saturday night.

You put your right arm in,
You put your right arm out,

You shake it a little, a little,
And turn yourself about.

You put your left arm in,
You put your left arm out,
You shake it a little, a little,
And turn yourself about.

You put your right leg in, etc.

You put your left leg in, etc.

You put your whole self in, etc.